I Could Eat You Up!

by JO HARPER

illustrated by KAY CHORAO

Holiday House / New York

Printed and Bound in Malaysia
The text typeface is Steam.
The art for this book was created in gouache and colored pencil
on hot press watercolor paper.
www.holidayhouse.com
First Edition
1 3 5 7 9 10 8 6 4 2

Library of Congress Cataloging~in~Publication Data
Harper, Jo.
I could eat you up! / by Jo Harper ; illustrations by Kay Chorao.— 1st ed.
p. cm.
Summary: Animal parents describe how much they love their children
by comparing them to food.
ISBN~13: 978-0-8234-1733-9 (hardcover)
ISBN~10: 0-8234-1733-6 (hardcover)
[1. Parent and child—Fiction. 2. Animals—Fiction.
3. Stories in rhyme.] I. Chorao, Kay, ill. II. Title.
PZ8.3.H2192Ico 2007
[E]—dc22
2005035638

For Rocky, Leslie,
and Jesse Giovanni
J. H.

For Sadie,
my little sweet pea
K. C.

You're a good egg.

You're a little milk jug.

You're a honeypot.

Please give me a hug.

You're my top banana.

You're my sugar lump.

I think you're a peach
'cause you're nice and plump.

You're my carrot curl.

You're my cat-nip tea.

You're my biscuit treat.

You're my black-eyed pea.

You're my juicy berry.

You're my sunflower seed.

You're my crunchy peanut.

You're what I need.
Oh, I could eat you all up!